First published in The Netherlands under the title *Vriendjes*

First published in the United States and Canada in 2013 by Lemniscaat USA LLC • New York
Distributed in the United States by Lemniscaat USA LLC • New York

Library of Congress Cataloging-in-Publication Data is available.
ISBN 13: 978-1-935954-23-1 (Hardcover)
Printing and binding: Worzalla, Stevens Point, WI USA
First U.S. edition

Friends

MIES VAN HOUT

LEMNISCAAT ROTTERDAM

play

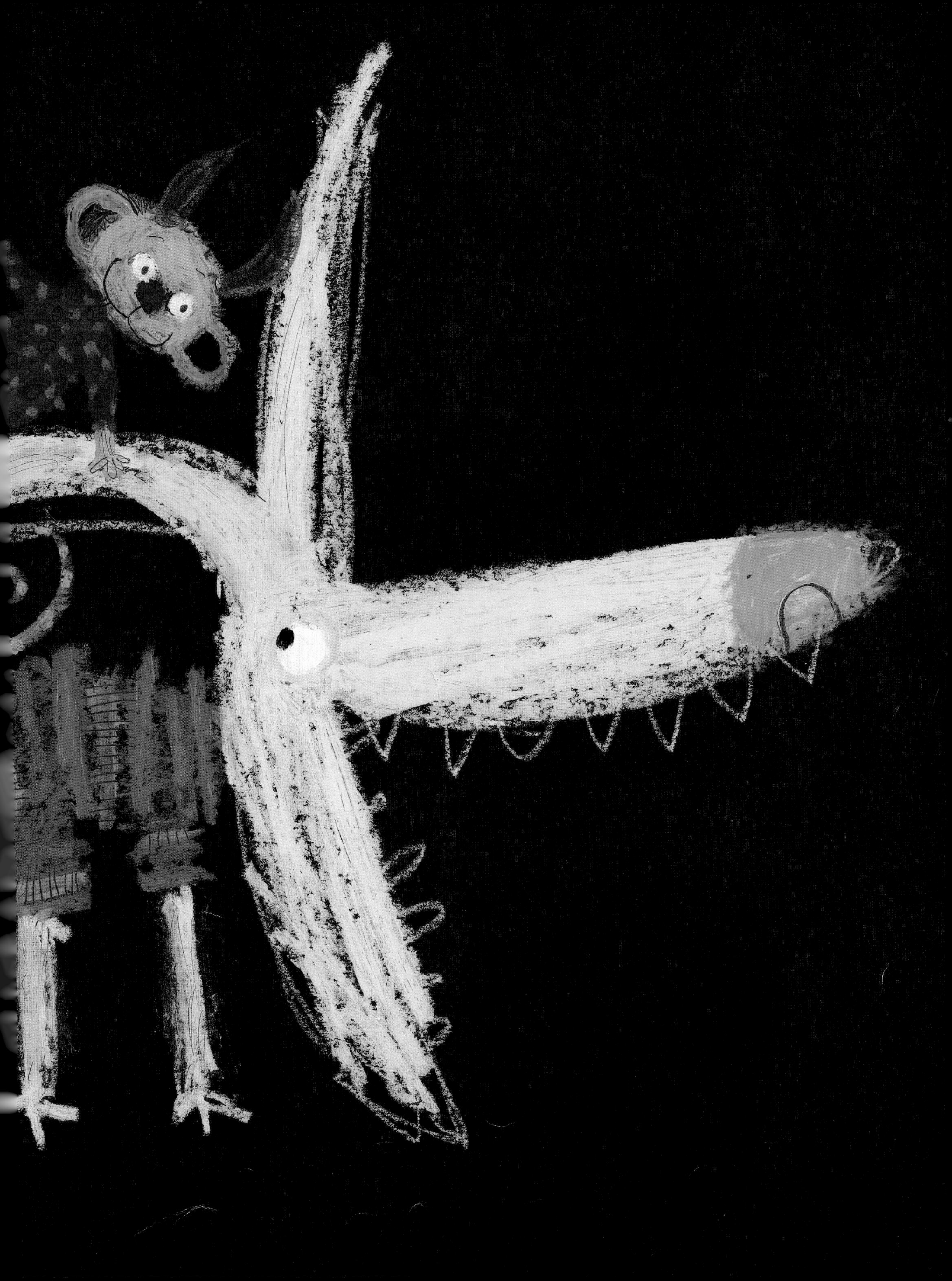

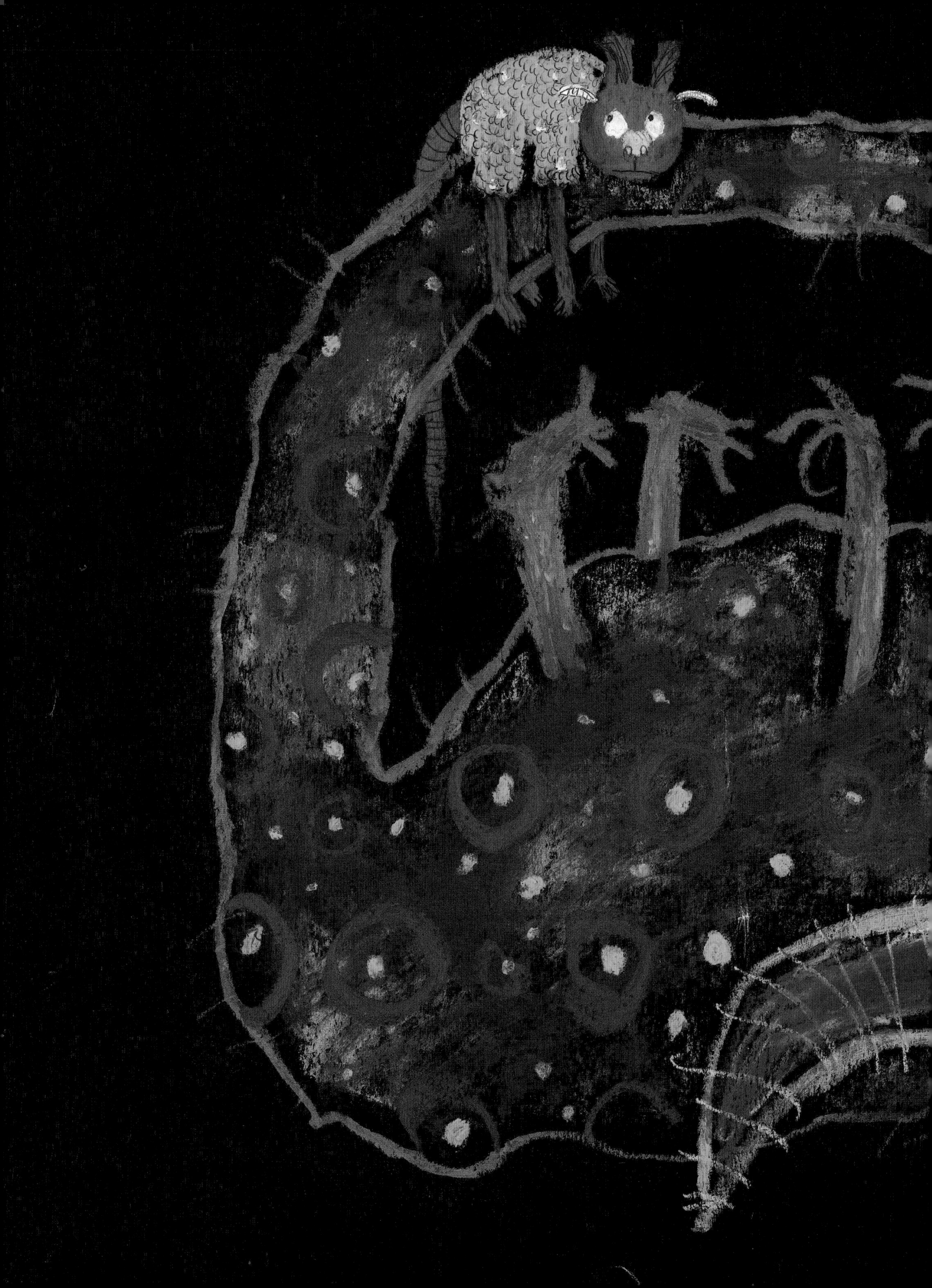

bore

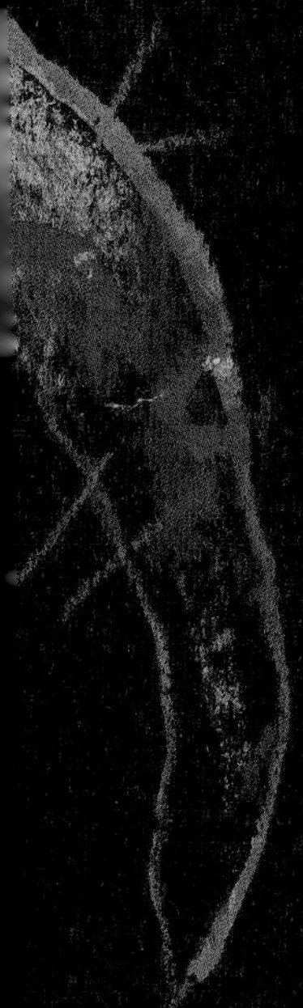

tease

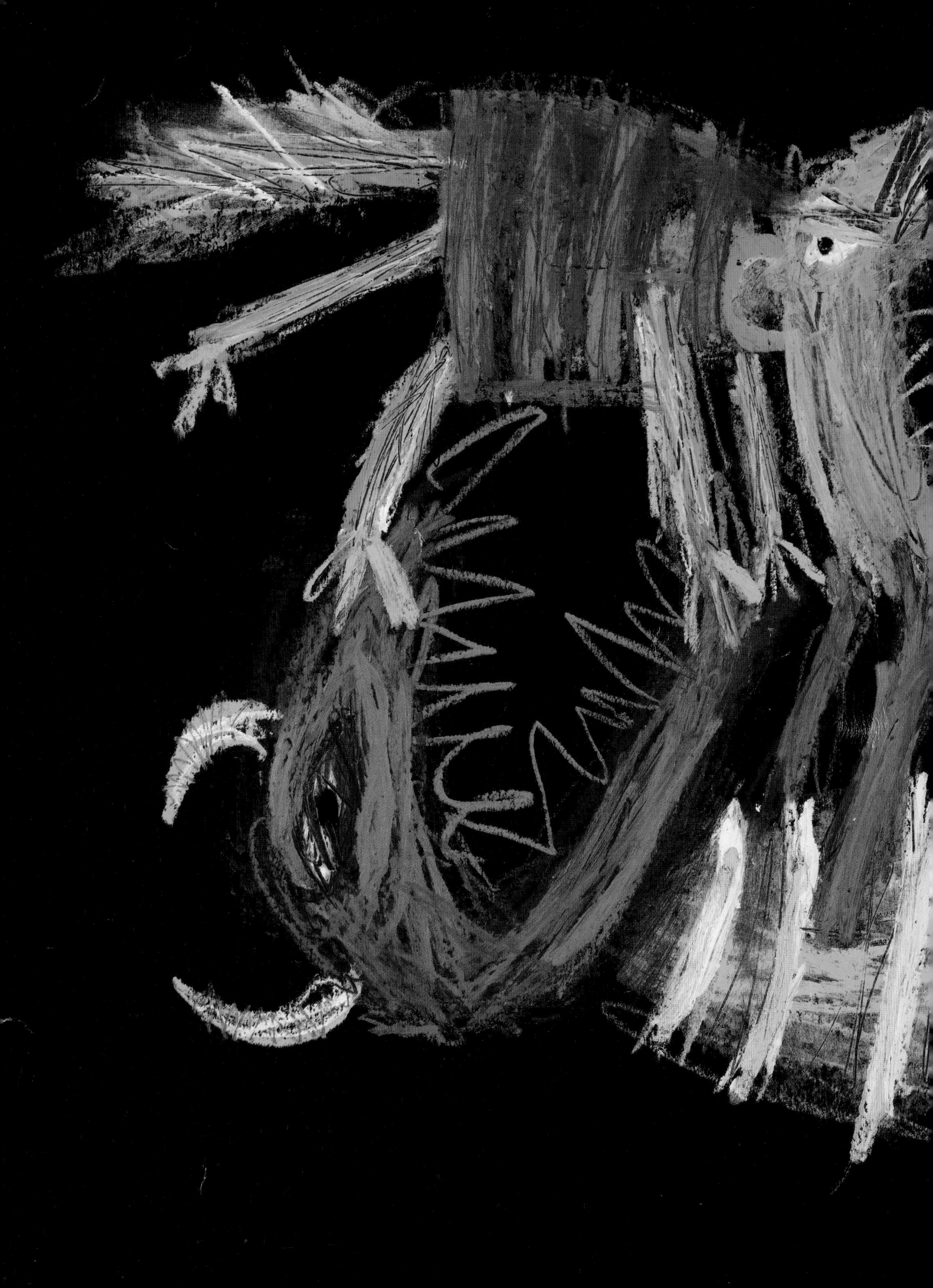

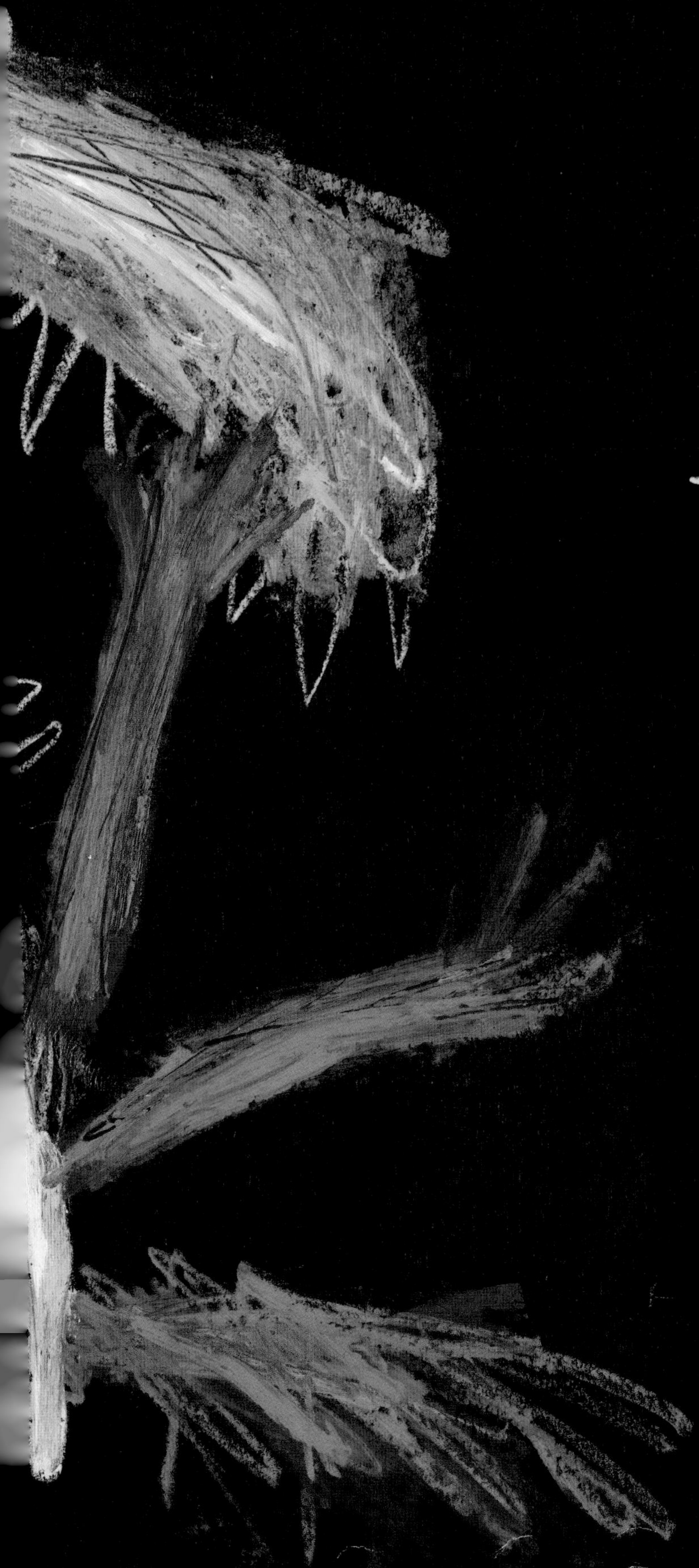

fight

Cry

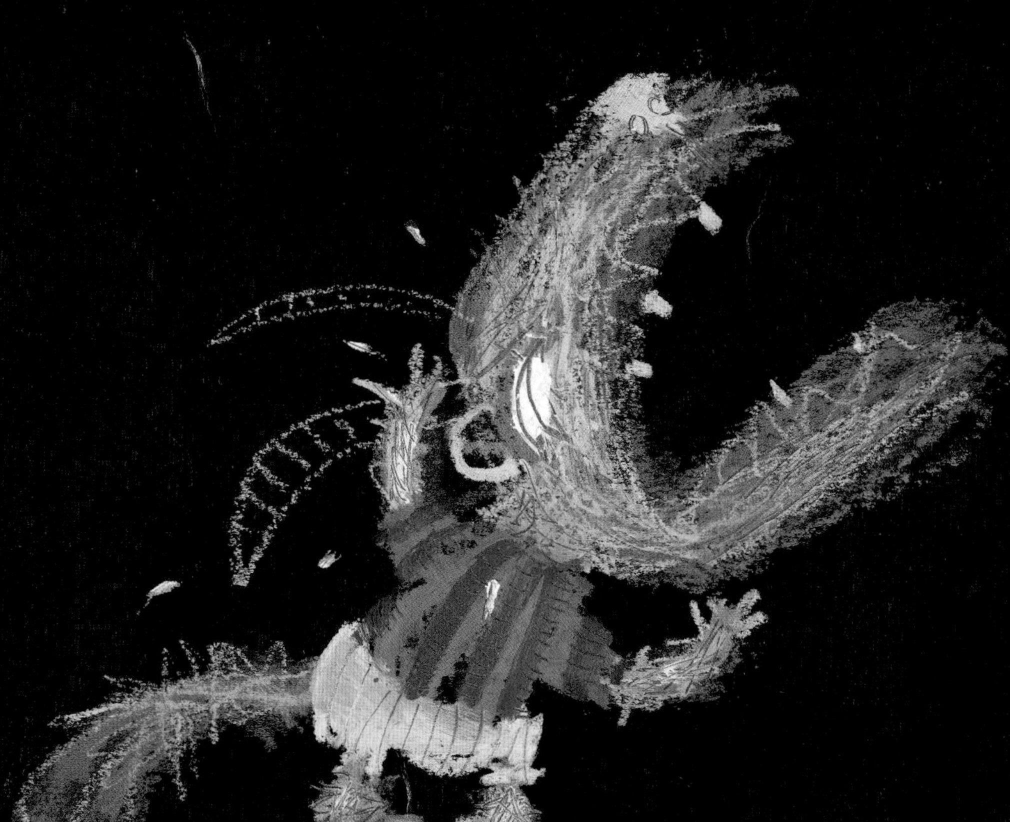

ignore

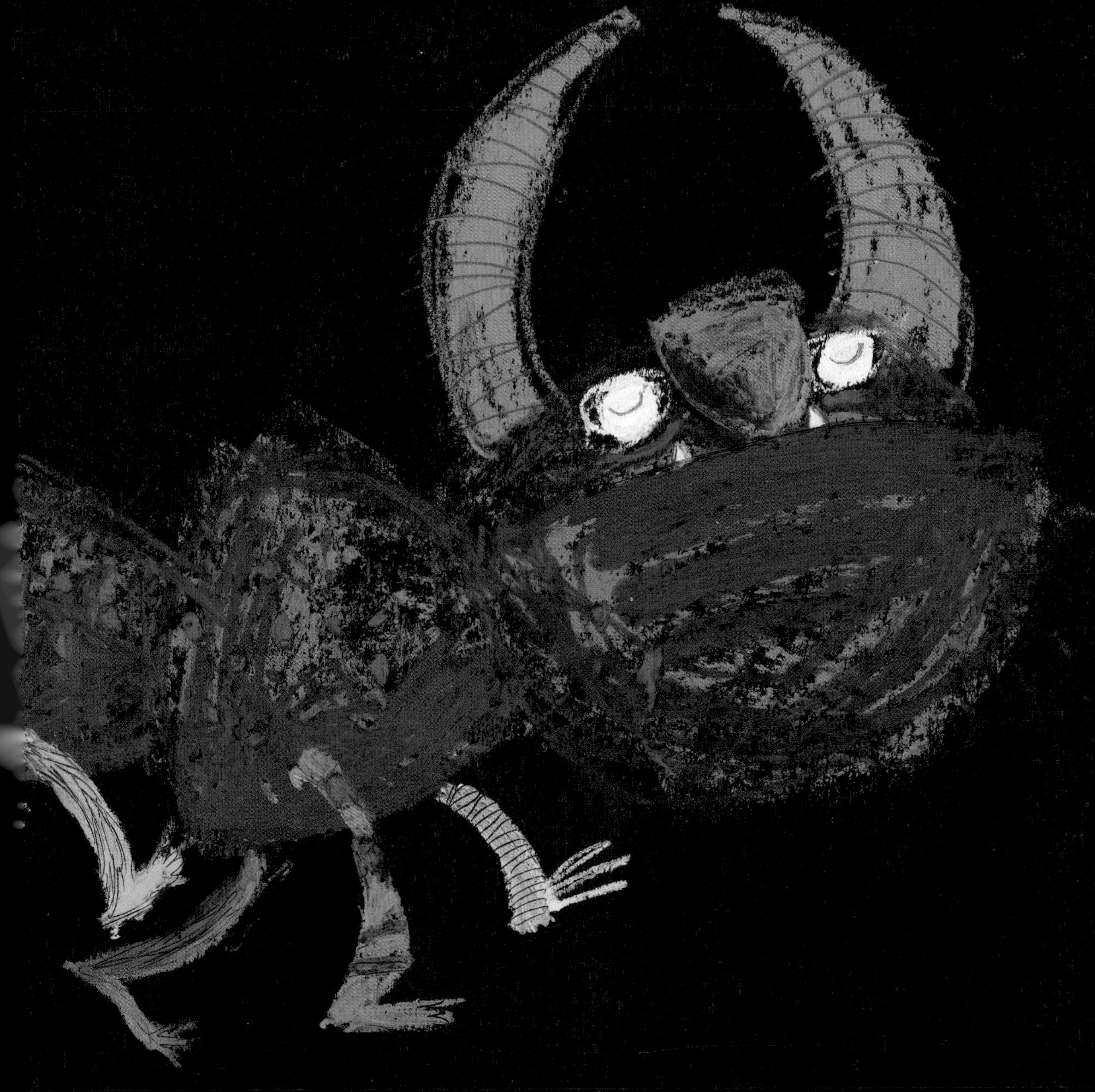

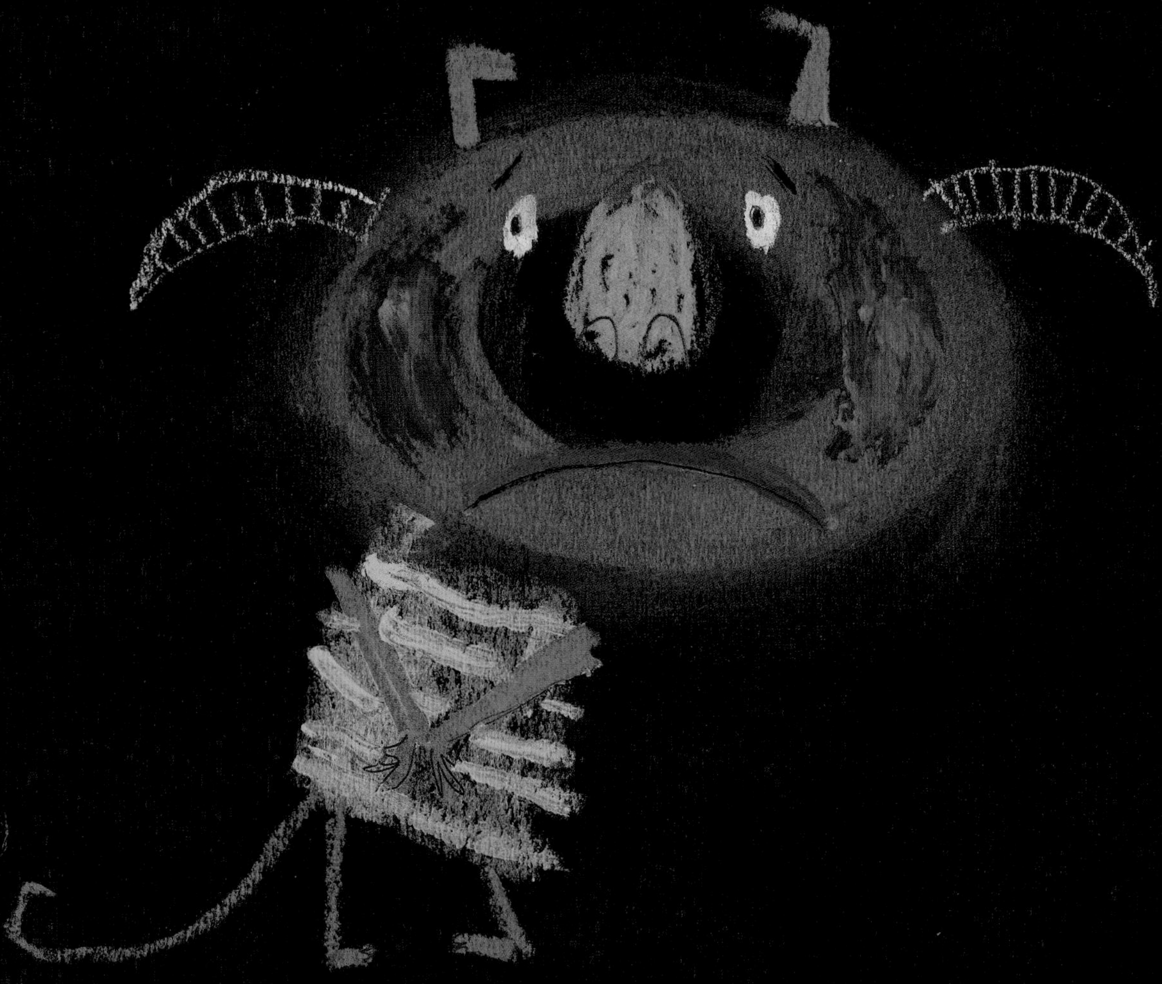

embarrass

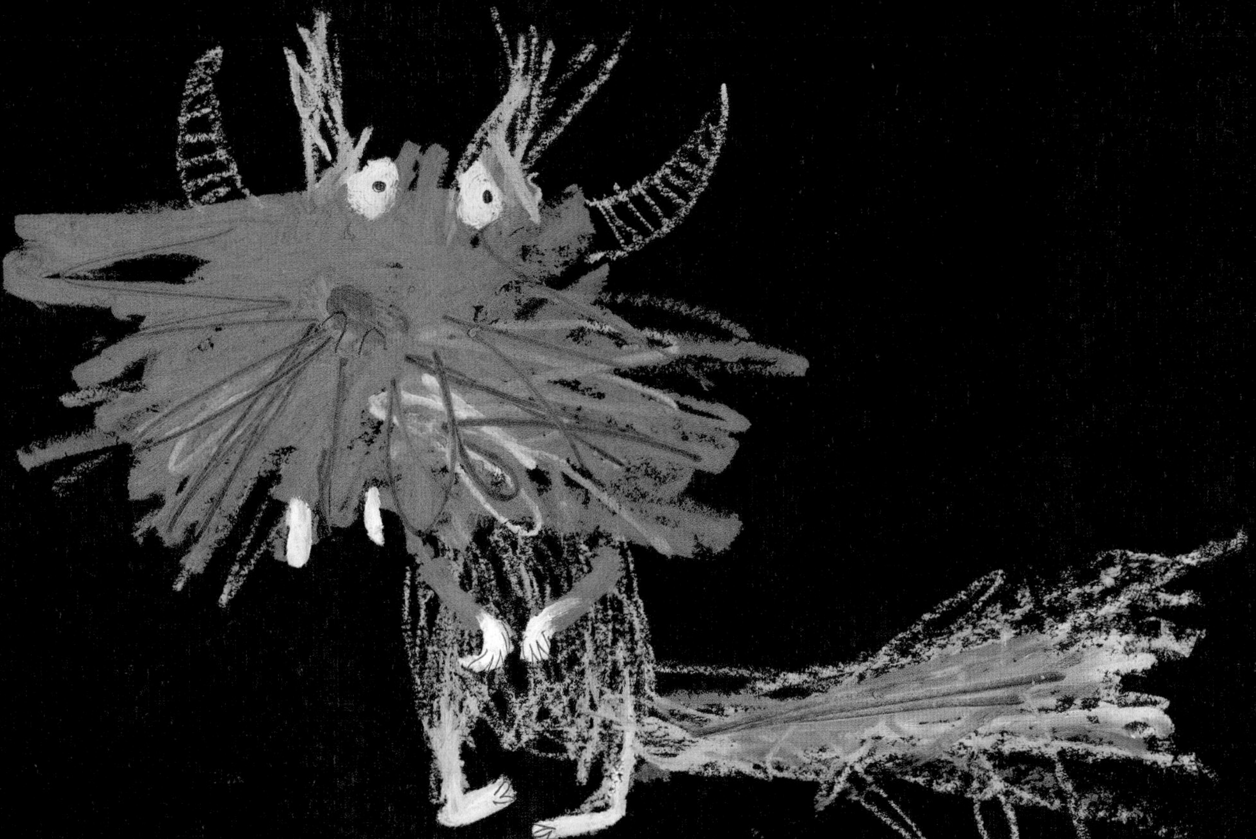

hope

make up

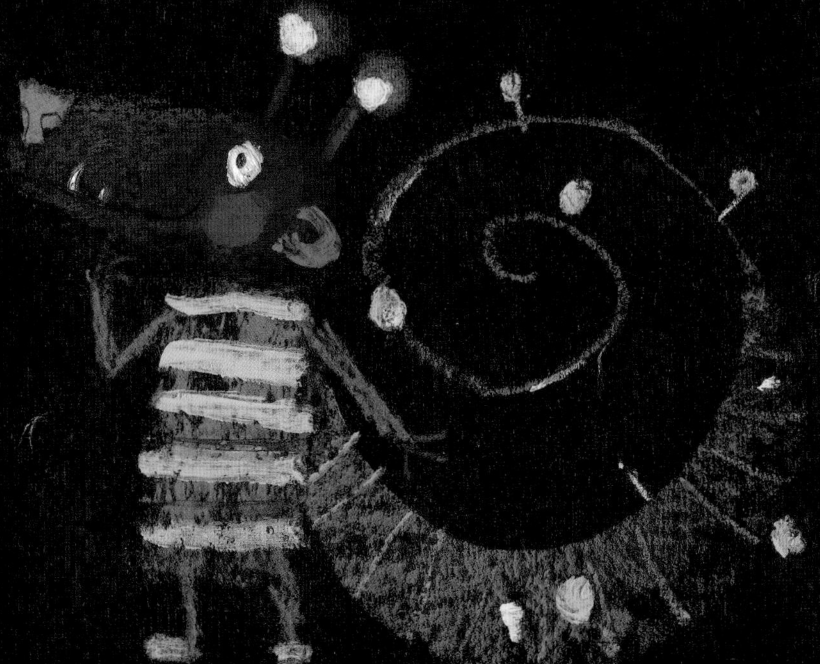

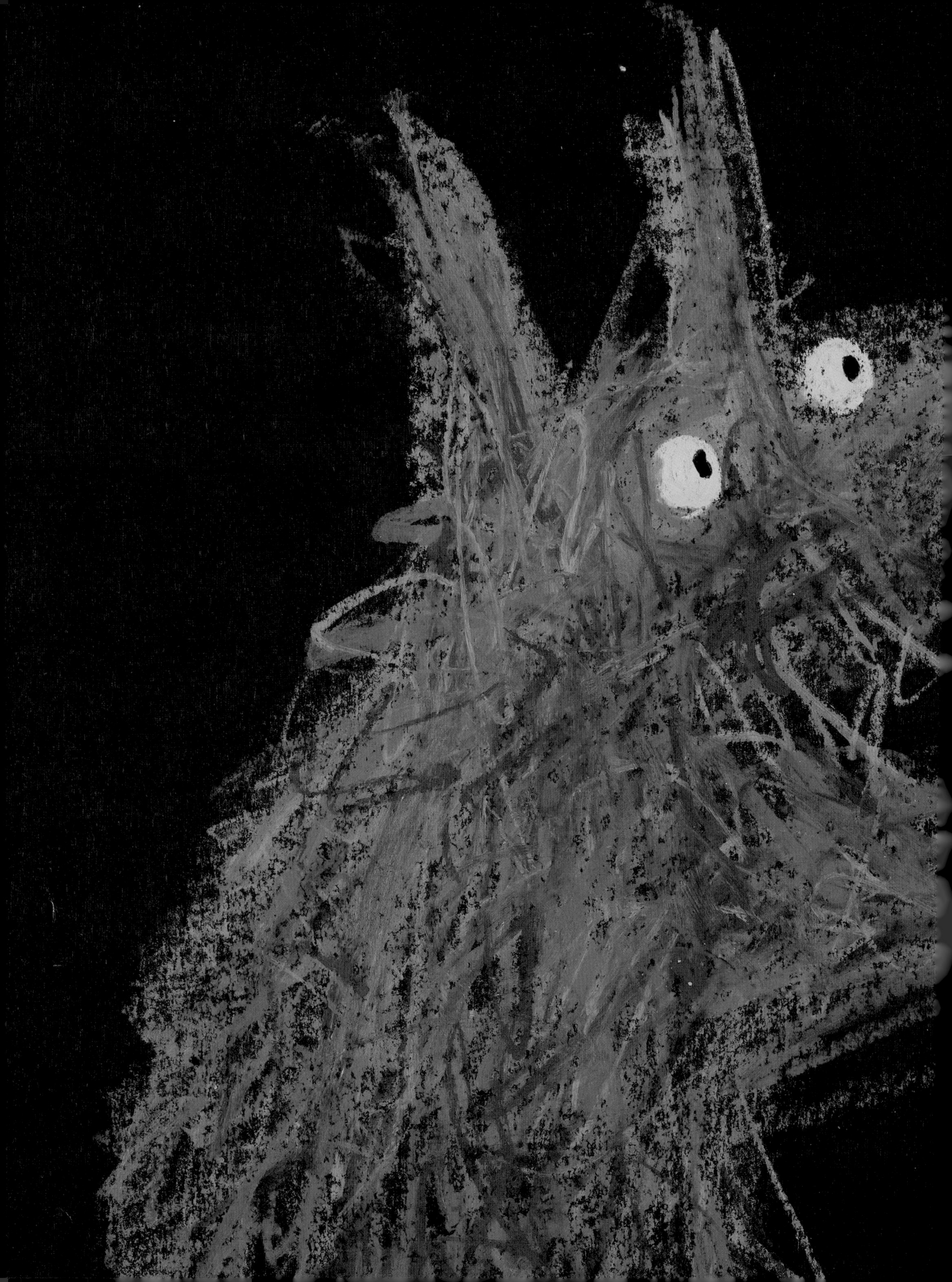

trust

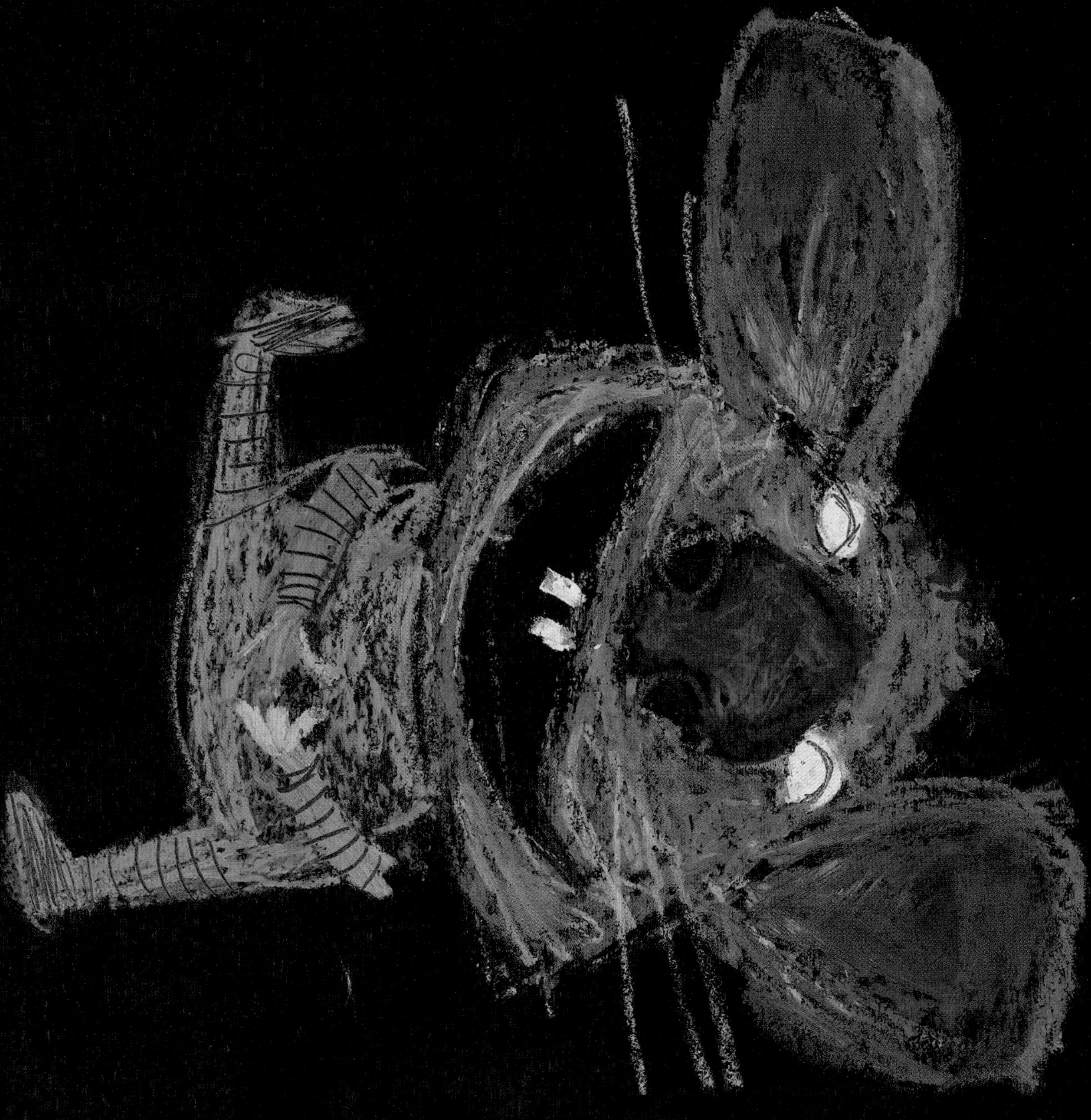

laugh

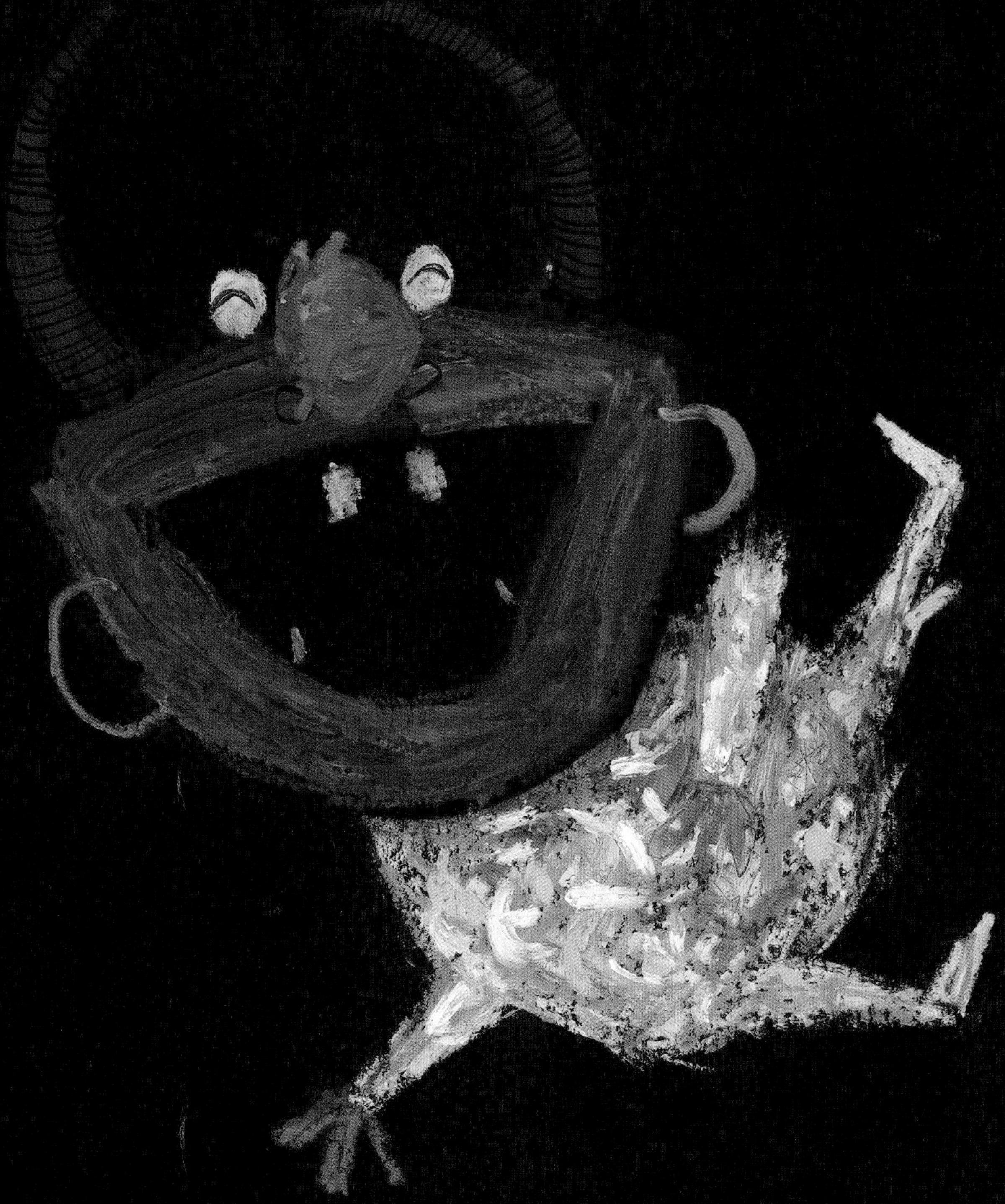

Cuddle

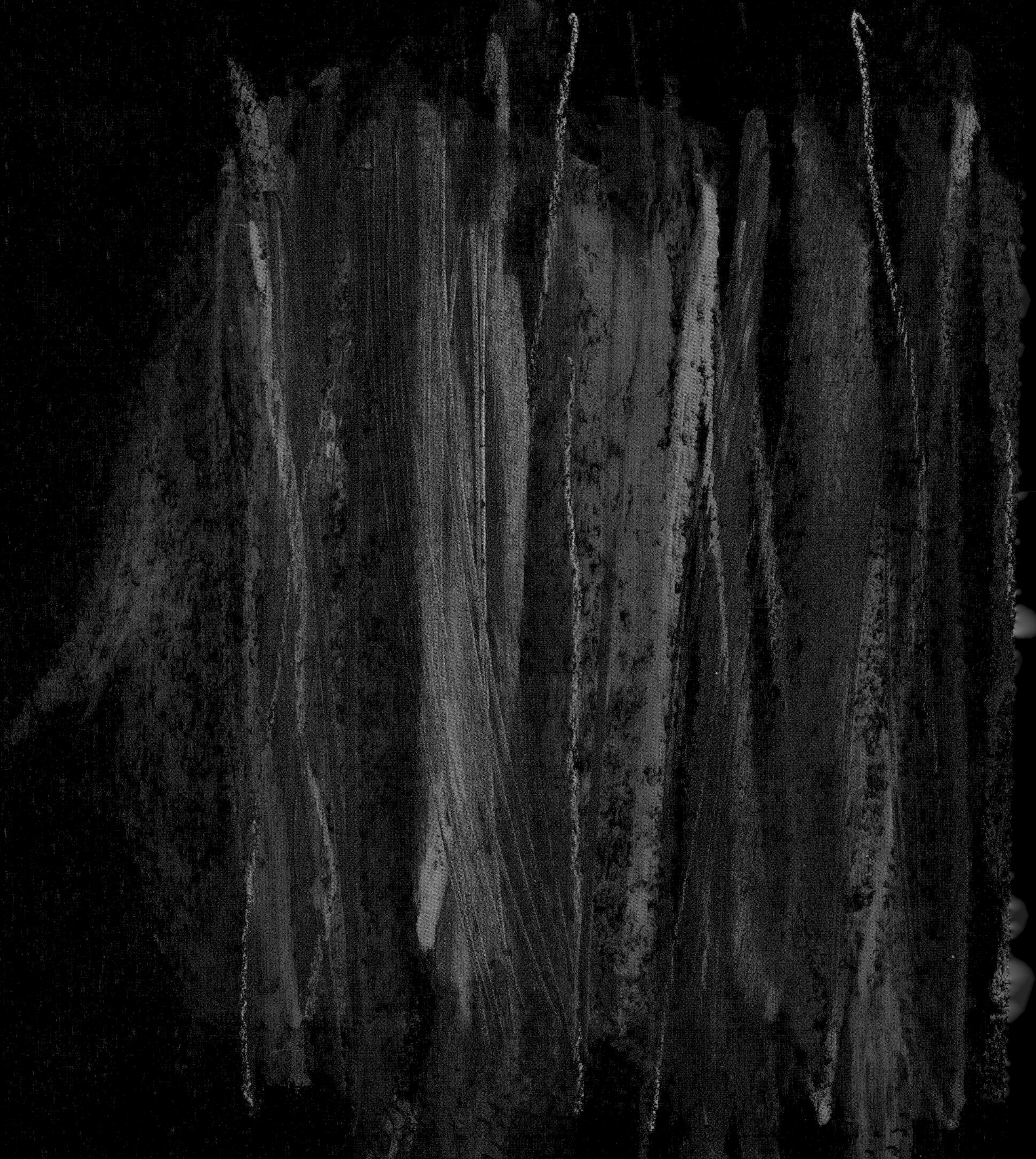

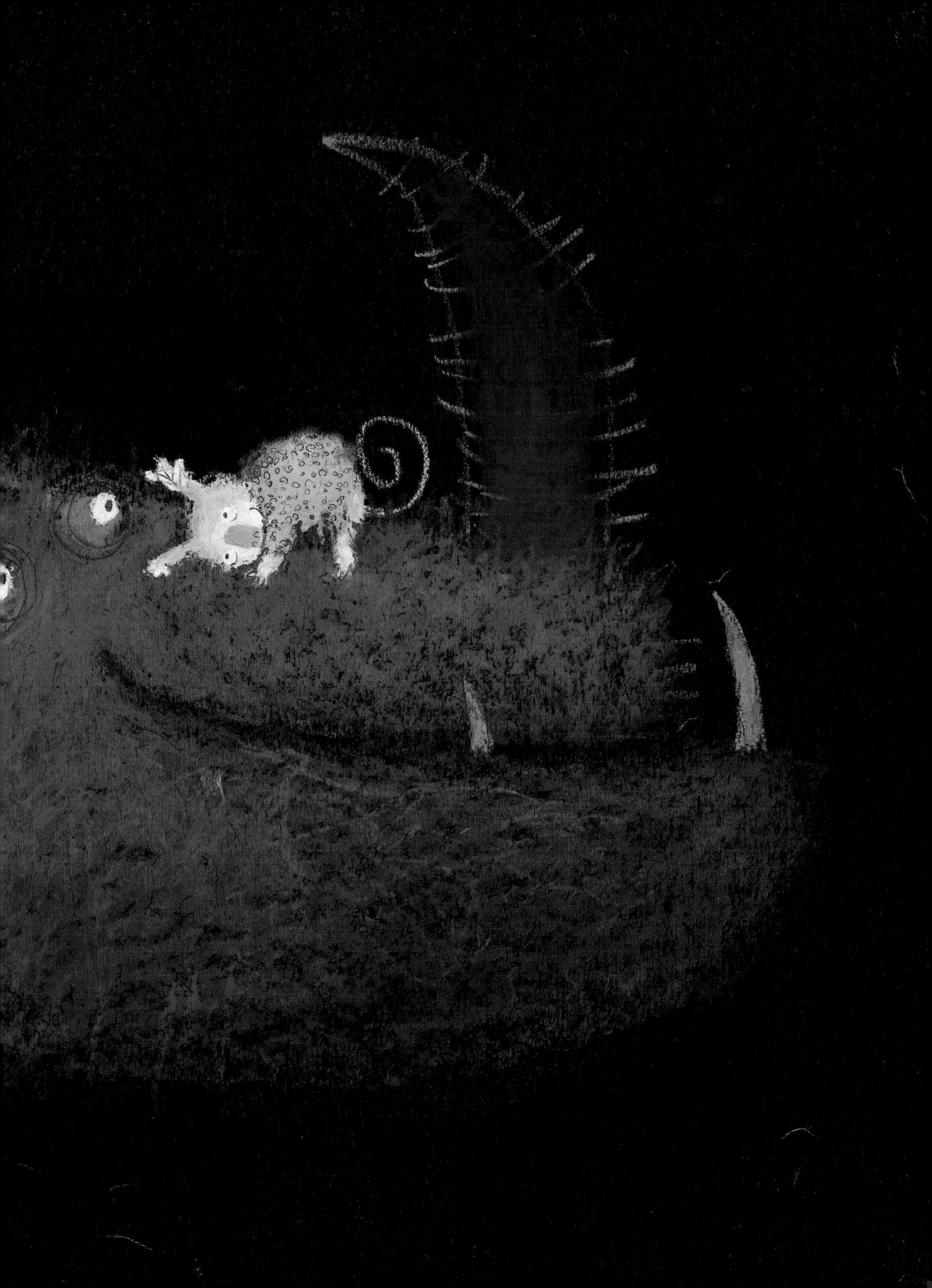